Six Hours

Pete Johnson

With illustrations by
Jen Collins

First published in 2014 in Great Britain by
Barrington Stoke Ltd
18 Walker Street, Edinburgh, EH3 7LP

www.barringtonstoke.co.uk

A CIP catalogue record for this book is available
from the British Library upon request

ISBN: 978-1-78112-363-8

Printed in China by Leo

Contents

Chapter 1
The Great Escape

Dominic was getting scared.

He looked around. It was the start of the exam in the hall. And everyone seemed to be writing – except him. Dominic couldn't write anything for one simple reason – he had forgotten every single thing he'd ever learned.

His brain had frozen up.

What on earth was happening? It didn't make any sense. History was Dominic's best subject. And he'd revised for this exam every night for weeks. But now ...

'You're a bit nervous, that's all,' he told himself. He picked up his pen. Only he couldn't hold on to it. His hands shook too much. His tummy hurt too. It felt like it was about to explode.

"I feel sick!" The words were yelled across the hall. So someone else was feeling groggy. Dominic turned round to see who it was.

A hot, blonde girl from Dominic's class was swinging her hand in the air. Lara.

Mr King was the teacher in charge. He rushed over to Lara. "How dare you shout out in an exam?" he hissed.

"But I've been waving my hand for ages," Lara said. "And I'm going to throw up any second."

Mr King spluttered a bit. "All right," he whispered. "You may go and see the school nurse. I shall speak to you later."

"I can't wait," Lara muttered.

Dominic couldn't help but smile. He'd never talk to a teacher like that. No wonder Lara was in trouble so often. She always had a lot to say for herself.

But after Lara had gone Dominic felt worse. He took some deep breaths. They didn't help. And now his head was spinning.

At last he raised his hand. Mr King stormed over and glared down at him.

"Please Sir, I feel ill," Dominic said.

"You too!" Mr King said with a heavy sigh. "All right, go and see the school nurse. I'll speak to you later as well."

As Dominic stumbled out of the hall, he could hardly see where he was going. But the weird thing was, as soon as he was outside he felt better. And by the time he reached the nurse's room, he didn't feel sick at all.

The nurse was thin and miserable looking, with very small, very sharp eyes. Right now, her eyes were fixed on Dominic as he walked up and down her room. Next she made him touch his toes. And then she took his pulse.

"It's normal," she said. "There's nothing wrong with you."

Dominic had to agree with her. He felt bursting with health now. But if he returned to the exam room he was sure his head would start to spin again and that horrible sick feeling would return too.

Then Lara staggered out from the loo at the back of the nurse's room. "I've puked up twice, Nurse," she announced. "I hope I haven't got any bits of carrot in my hair."

Dominic just stopped himself from laughing out loud.

But the nurse snapped at Lara. "Show me your tongue."

"Feels a bit rude to stick my tongue out at you." Lara grinned.

The nurse didn't grin back. Instead, she felt Lara's head and then took her pulse.

"If I could just lie still on your couch I'm sure I'll feel better in a few hours," Lara said.

"You're better now," the nurse said. "You both are."

Then one of the secretaries came in to say that the nurse was needed upstairs.

The nurse sighed. "I haven't had a moment to myself this morning."

"It's so annoying when people are ill, isn't it?" Lara said.

The nurse glared at her. "I shall return in a few moments with a teacher to take you both back into your exam," she said. Then she swept out.

Lara lay down on the couch. "That woman is a total nightmare," she said. "Anyone else would have believed me. I thought that bit about me having carrots in my hair was pretty good."

"So you're not really ill?" Dominic asked.

"Well, doh, of course not," Lara said. Then she sat up. "But you're a bit of a swot, so why are you here?"

Dominic shook his head. "I've been revising for weeks, only today ..." He hesitated.

"Yeah, go on?" Lara sat up.

"The questions just went round and round in my head," Dominic told her. "It made me feel so dizzy that I forgot everything. I could just about remember my name."

"You total saddo," Lara said. Then she jumped to her feet. "See you."

Dominic looked at her in surprise. "Where are you going?"

"Escaping," she said.

"You're walking out of school?" Dominic was shocked.

"Of course." Lara looked at him like he was a bit soft in the head. "Come too if you like."

Dominic was so shocked he couldn't speak at first. "But what ... what will we do?"

"Just chill," Lara said.

'This is like a dream,' Dominic thought. The hottest girl in his class – in the universe – was offering to chill with him. Nerd Boy.

That nickname used to follow Dominic everywhere. Then, one day, a boy shouted it out as he was arriving at school. Dominic just snapped and started to fight the boy. He lost the fight but the nickname faded away too.

But inside, Dominic still felt like Nerd Boy. And he'd given up hope of any girl ever being interested in him.

"So are you coming?" Lara asked. Then she rolled her eyes. "No, of course you're not because you're soooo boring, aren't you?"

"Er ..." Dominic began.

"Forget it, I'm gone," Lara said.

"No wait," Dominic yelled. "I'm in." He enjoyed the flash of surprise that crossed Lara's face. He'd sort of impressed her.

"OK," she said. "Follow me. We'll get our bags first. And remember, just walk about as if you own the place. Whatever you do, don't look scared or guilty." She opened the door. "It's all clear."

Lara marched over to where their bags were, just outside the exam room. She grabbed her bag. Dominic found his too.

"The secretary in the office goes off for a coffee about now," Lara said. "But I'd better check. You wait inside there." She pointed at the male staff loo. "I'll knock three times when the coast is clear."

Dominic went into the loo and looked around. It was smaller and posher than the boys' loo. But it had the same pongy stink. Teachers make smells like everyone else. That thought cheered him up a bit.

But it felt so odd to be hiding in here. And was Dominic really going to skive off? He'd be in so much trouble at school, and with his mum and ...

No, he couldn't do it.

But he couldn't go back to that exam either. He was totally stuck.

"Are you deaf?"

The loo door swung open so suddenly it made Dominic jump. Lara was standing outside glaring at him.

"Sorry," he began. "I didn't hear –"

"No time to chat now," Lara snapped. "No one's about so I'll leave first. You follow me a few seconds later. And remember, look confident at all times."

Dominic watched Lara stride past the school office. The next moment she was out of the door leading to the playground. She'd done it. She'd escaped.

Now it was his turn. And he was going to do it. He'd decided.

So Dominic walked very fast past the office, his heart beating wildly. He was at the door. He was going to get away with it. But then he heard a voice. "Dominic, you shouldn't be here now."

He whirled round.

The secretary was clicking towards him on her high heels. She had a mug of coffee in her hand.

Now what could he do?

Chapter 2
Return to Sender

Dominic hesitated.

"Dominic, what are you doing?" the secretary went on.

Dominic began to panic. What could he say? Nothing. He decided there was only one thing he could do.

So he ran out of the door.

Then he pelted at top speed across the playground and charged out of the school gates.

Lara was waiting for him. "Why are you running?" she demanded. "I told you to –"

"The secretary," he began, still out of breath. "She yelled out my name and then asked me –"

"But you don't ever run!" Lara said. "That's the very worst thing you could have done."

"Sorry," Dominic murmured.

Lara shook her head. "You acted like a total nerd."

There it was again – the word he hated and could never escape from. "Don't call me a nerd," he said.

"If you act like a nerd, I'll call you one," Lara snapped.

"Well, you shouldn't have asked me to come along," Dominic said.

"I didn't," she retorted.

"Yes you did."

"I felt sorry for you, that's all."

Dominic reddened with shame. She made him sound like a lost puppy.

"You'd better go back," Lara said. "You'll be all right. You're such a good boy –"

"I can't go back to that exam," Dominic cried. "I'd rather swallow my own bogies."

"That's disgusting!" Lara replied, but a faint smile flickered across her face. "OK," she said. "Let's go."

Then she walked off so fast Dominic had to half-run to keep up with her.

"So where are we going?" he asked.

"I've got to post something."

"There's a post box at the end of this road," Dominic said, trying to be helpful.

But Lara walked right past the post box.

"Hey, you've missed it," Dominic said. "It's back there."

Lara whirled round. "I'm not posting it there."

'Why ever not?' Dominic thought. Then he noticed something else – it looked as if there were tears in her eyes. Should he say something? Ask her if she was all right? He wished he knew more about girls. But they were a complete mystery to him, and mainly just ignored him.

Lara turned round again. "Come on," she said, "walk faster."

"Where are we going?" Dominic asked as he increased his pace.

"Millets Drive. Blake Powell's house."

Dominic was about to ask why on earth they were going there when he remembered something. "You used to go out with Blake," he said.

Lara nodded and went red.

"But you've just broken up with him, haven't you?"

Lara nodded again, and went even redder.

Dominic remembered something else. Lara was supposed to have said some nasty stuff about Blake. Dominic never found out exactly what, but he knew the school was buzzing with it. And then Blake dumped her. But that was her own fault, so Dominic wasn't going to feel sorry for her.

"Why," Dominic asked, "are we going to see him?"

"I told you," Lara said.

"No you didn't."

Lara glared at him. "We're going to post all the stupid, pathetic, moronic presents he gave me through his letterbox."

"Did he ask for them back?" Dominic asked.

"No," Lara said. "But I don't want them."

Dominic wondered why she didn't just put them in the bin. He was confused. Then he remembered that she'd been crying before.

Was she upset about the break-up? And was

she hoping to see Blake again? But Blake would

be at school. Unless he was chilling today too.

What was going on?

Lara stopped outside the first house

in Millets Drive. She dug into her bag and

produced some little furry toys, a necklace and

a ring. "All cheap," she said. "He was so

tight-fisted." Next she started posting them

into his letterbox.

All except one.

A huge white toy dog, that wouldn't fit into the letterbox.

"Leave it on the mat," Dominic suggested.

"No," Lara said, and she rang the doorbell. Then she threw the giant toy at Dominic. "Just say Lara asked you to return this."

"Wha–at?" Dominic said.

"It won't take you a second," Lara said. "Even you can't mess it up." And with that, she started to walk away.

Dominic stood gasping with shock. And that's when he felt something dribbling down his chin.

Not again! He'd had so many nosebleeds in the last few months. His mum said they were very common in boys his age, but of all the moments for it to happen! He balanced the toy dog under his chin and reached into his pocket for his hankie.

At that very moment, the front door opened.

A woman jumped back in alarm when she saw Dominic bleeding on her step. Then she noticed all the presents on the mat. "Did you just do that?" she demanded.

"Well, it wasn't exactly me –" Dominic began.

"And who are you?" the woman interrupted.

"I'm Lara," Dominic said into his very red hankie. Then, when he saw the woman looked even more alarmed, he added, "I mean, I'm not Lara, of course, I'm ... well it doesn't matter who I am. You won't have heard of me. Not many people have, but I meant to say Lara asked me to return this dog." He pressed the dog into the woman's hands. "And it just bit me – so be careful." Then he sped away.

The nosebleed didn't last long. And when Dominic told Lara what he'd said she fell about laughing.

"Respect!" she said.

Dominic looked at her.

"No really," she went on. "What you said about the dog biting you, that's funny."

"Well I can be quite funny sometimes," Dominic muttered. "I mean, in my head I say some very amusing things. It's just I don't often say them out loud."

"Well you should," Lara said.

It was one of the best moments in Dominic's life. A really hot girl was smiling at him. Nerd Boy.

And then his mobile rang.

It was his mum.

Chapter 3
Just Chilling

"Don't answer it," Lara said at once.

"I wasn't going to," said Dominic.

"And switch it off," she ordered.

She really was incredibly bossy, but Dominic did as she said.

"The school must have rung my house already," he said.

"Of course they have," Lara said. "You couldn't have acted more obvious, running out like that. So will your mum go mad?"

"She'll totally freak out," Dominic said, with a gloomy nod.

"What will your dad do?" Lara asked.

"Not much. He's dead."

"Oh ..." Lara's voice fell away.

"But I've got a step-dad," Dominic said. "He loves exams. He goes on and on about how important they are, and how they'll decide my whole future. Nothing's more important than exams, he says. He'll go ape when he finds out what I've done."

"But you haven't done anything wrong," Lara said.

"Yes I have," said Dominic. "I've skived off."

"Only in a very small way," Lara said. "It was a mock exam, so all you've done is leave school at 10 a.m. rather than 4 p.m. So you walked out six hours early. Well, six hours is nothing. Every teenager should be allowed

36

to have six hours off, to just chill. In fact, I'd make it a law. Once a month we are allowed a chill day." Then she added, "Look, to stop your parents worrying, you could always send them a little message."

"What will I say?" Dominic asked.

"Two words," Lara said. "Just chill."

"They won't understand that," Dominic said.

"Well at least they'll know you're still breathing," she said. "Go on, do it."

It was like a dare. And Dominic was keen to impress Lara, so he texted his mum, 'Just chill.'

Then he grinned. "She'll be puzzling over that all day."

"Give her something to do," Lara said. "And now shall we go to the seaside?"

Dominic stared at her. It was the middle of February. It was cold and it was drizzling with rain.

"It's only two stops away on the train," she went on. "And don't forget, today we're free to go wherever we want."

"OK," said Dominic. "Let's go to the seaside."

Chapter 4
On the Beach

The last time Dominic had been here, the beach was swarming with people. Today it was deserted and it only seemed half-alive. There were just a few seagulls flying in circles above their heads. The sea itself looked grey and unfriendly.

"This is quality," Dominic said. He wasn't being serious.

But Lara replied, "Yeah, isn't it great? And we've got the whole beach to ourselves, with no one to annoy us." Then she pointed. "Do you see that ice cream van down there?"

"Yeah."

"Well, I'll have an ice cream with two flakes," she said. "And don't forget to get one for yourself."

"You're too kind," Dominic replied. "And what are you going to do?"

"Wait here for you," she said.

Dominic walked fast, but it still took him over ten minutes to reach the van. A bored-looking boy sat inside. "You're my first customer today," he said.

"Do I get extra ice cream for that?" Dominic asked.

The boy didn't answer, but he handed Dominic two huge ice creams.

Dominic strolled back. He saw Lara stretched out on the sand, as if it were a beautiful summer's day. And then he saw something else.

A huge Alsatian was galloping across the beach, barking in a very angry way. An Alsatian in a bad mood is never a happy sight. And this one was making straight for Dominic.

Dominic began to run. This was not a great idea as the Alsatian just upped its speed too. He could hear the thump of its paws behind him. He ran harder still, but it was too late. In seconds, the Alsatian was right in front of him and going crazy.

"Nice dog," Dominic cried. "I'm your friend."

But the dog didn't seem keen on new friends. He was far more interested in attacking Dominic's trousers. In the end

Dominic lost his balance. He toppled forward and both ice creams flew from his grip and landed on the sand with a mighty slurp.

At the same time a voice bellowed, "Kelly!" and a woman in a grey suit strode towards them. The Alsatian shrank back straight away. "I'm so sorry," the woman said to Dominic. She helped him to his feet and brushed the sand off him. "Kelly wouldn't have done you any harm," she explained. "It's just she loves ice cream."

And Kelly was, at that very moment, busy licking up both ice creams. Before the woman left, she insisted on giving Dominic the money for two more.

When she had gone, Dominic went back to Lara, who was falling about laughing.

"Stop it," he said, "that was a hairy moment."

But Lara had such a brilliant laugh he couldn't help joining in.

"Do you know what I'm going to do now?" he asked.

"Amaze me," Lara said.

"This." He flung off his shoes and socks, rolled up his trousers and leaped into the sea.

Then he started to kick and jump about. "It's freezing but it's brilliant," he yelled.

"You're mad," Lara yelled back.

In fact, Dominic did feel a bit mad, but in a good way. He could really be himself now – the secret, funny person he was in his head. So he went on splashing about and called, "Come on, you can't come to the seaside and not get your feet wet. Or are you scared?"

"Me, scared?" Lara jumped into the sea too. And soon they were giggling and laughing and having a water fight. Then Lara flopped down on the sand. "I'll say one thing about you," she

said. "You're the world champion at making me laugh."

Dominic had never had a bigger compliment from a girl – from anyone.

Later they strolled off to play on the slot machines in the arcade. No one else was there at first. But then two boys slouched in. They didn't play on the machines, they just stood and stared at Lara and then at Dominic.

'They think I'm her boyfriend,' Dominic thought. He felt quite proud. He wasn't her boyfriend, of course. But it was great they thought he was.

Neither Lara nor Dominic won any money and they soon got bored. So they armed themselves with ice creams and returned to the beach. Lara started to make a sandcastle while rain clouds hovered just above their heads. Then after a while she stopped and said, "I wish we could stay here forever. I wouldn't miss a single person."

"Not even your friends?" Dominic asked.

"What friends?" The words burst out of her. "You've heard the rumours about me, haven't you?"

Dominic didn't know what to say. "I did hear that you've been –" he began.

"That I've been slagging off Blake," Lara interrupted. "I bet even you knew about that."

Dominic didn't like the 'even you' but he still nodded.

"I didn't say one word of it, you know," she said. "It was all made up by one of my so-called friends." She turned to look at Dominic. "No one believes me. And I bet you don't."

He hesitated but only for a moment.

"I believe you all right," he said.

Lara shook her head. "You don't need to pretend ..."

"I'm not pretending," he said.

Lara looked away. "Blake never believed me. I told him over and over I didn't say any of that mean, nasty stuff. He was my boyfriend so he should have listened to me – not them. And now I hate him."

"Maybe later –" Dominic began.

"Just hearing his name makes me want to puke," Lara said.

There was silence then, broken only by the seagulls making their strange, bleating cries in the sky.

"I thought," Lara went on at last, "if I could just find out who started the rumours –"

"Yeah, that's what you've got to do," Dominic interrupted.

"Well, last night I did just that."

"You know who it is?" he said.

"It's Vanessa, my now ex best friend," Lara said. Her voice was flat.

Dominic was shocked. "Are you sure?"

"I'm sure," she said, and her voice was flatter still. "Never suspected her for a second.

But last night I worked it all out. And all of a sudden it made sense."

"But why would Vanessa want to do that?" Dominic asked.

"Oh, why do you think?" Now Lara sounded fed-up and impatient.

Dominic thought for a moment. "Did Vanessa want to go out with Blake?"

"Of course she did," Lara said. "And now she will. You'll see."

"But you've got to tell everyone the truth," Dominic cried.

Lara's eyes narrowed and darkened. "Vanessa's very, very clever – she fools everyone with her 'nice' act. Even me until last night."

"But you're so popular and cool," Dominic said.

"Oh yeah, and being one of the cool kids meant everything to me," Lara told him. "It was all I could think about. Nothing else mattered. But now ... do you want to hear something truly, truly weird?"

"Course I do."

"At first," Lara said, "when I found out what Vanessa had done I was so mad I couldn't speak. Then I sent her such an evil text. 'Suck on that, you total cow,' I thought. But later …"

"Yeah?" Dominic prompted.

"I realised I just didn't care about any of it. And my friends could stick it. So could school –"

"And don't forget family," Dominic interrupted. "The ones who call you their little star."

Lara looked at him in total horror. "Your family call you that? You should report them for child abuse."

"My step-dad started it and now I can't stop them," Dominic rushed on. "They won't believe I'm nothing special at school. Good at History – well I was until today – but just average at everything else. No, they want me to be one of life's winners. My step-dad's the worst. He never stops yattering on about it. And when I turned over the exam paper today, all I could hear was his voice in my head, yelling at me. And that's when my brain just seized up."

"Your step-dad should be put down," Lara said. "And I'd be very happy to do it."

They went on comparing notes about friends and family until Dominic looked at his watch and saw it was well after four o'clock.

Slowly they got to their feet.

And even more slowly, they walked off the beach.

Chapter 5
Another Shock

The train pulled into the station.

"Isn't it grim to be home?" Dominic said. "So, how many detentions do you think we'll get tomorrow?"

"I got three in one day one time," Lara said. "That's my record so far."

"Bet you'll smash that tomorrow," Dominic said. "And so will I. Not that I ever got three detentions in one day before."

"Have you even had one?" Lara smiled.

"Yeah, yeah," Dominic said. "I must have."

"Well, whatever happens," Lara said, "you're going to stand up to your mum and step-dad from now on. You have to tell them you can only do your best and you're not their little star."

"And you," he told her, "have got to stop thinking about Vanessa and Blake."

"Oh I've done that already, I told you," Lara said. "I don't need anyone. I'm as tough as they come."

Before they got off the train, they gave each other their mobile numbers.

'Like you do at the end of a holiday,' Dominic thought. 'And then you never hear from them again.' He felt pretty gloomy as they set off in different directions. He stopped and stared after Lara, until he couldn't see her any more. He wished he'd taken some pictures. Already, this day seemed as far away as a dream.

He trudged home.

He opened his front door. This was the part he'd dreaded the most. His heart was pounding. Now his mum and step-dad would make such a big fuss and go on and on at him.

His step-dad saw him first. He stormed over. "Have you any idea how worried your mother has been?" he demanded.

Dominic stood fixed to the spot. "I sent her a text," he said.

"Some rubbish," his step-dad said.

"It was what I did," Dominic said. "I had a little holiday from my life and just chilled." Even now he couldn't help smiling as he said it.

"You took a little holiday!" his step-dad spluttered. "But you can't just –"

"Dominic!" His mum flew over to him. "We've been so worried, love," she cried. Then she noticed the remains of blood on his face. "Oh no, what's happened to you?" Her face was twisted with concern. Even his step-dad looked a bit worried.

"It's all right, Mum," Dominic said. I had one of my nosebleeds, that's all."

"Your son has just told me he strolled out of his exam to take a little holiday from his life," his step-dad yelled. "Can you believe that?"

Mum looked at Dominic for a moment. "You really shouldn't have walked out of your exam," she said. Then, to Dominic's surprise, she said, "Still, it's not the end of the world."

"He's missed an exam!" his step-dad cried. He folded his arms and his eyes narrowed with anger.

"He's safe, that's the important thing," his mum said.

Dominic gazed at her in total shock.

"We'll talk about it later," she went on. "Now, I expect you're hungry."

"Starving," said Dominic.

"Well," she said, "you go upstairs and clean up and we'll have something for you when you come down."

Dominic left, but listened at the door for a moment.

"You're not going to let him get away with it," his step-dad said.

"The school will punish him tomorrow, but it was only a mock exam," his mum replied. Her voice dropped to a whisper. "Did you see how pale and tired he looked? I worry we're putting too much pressure on him. Maybe we should ease off him a bit."

Dominic's step-dad was obviously too angry to reply and just thumped away. Dominic felt like cheering. His mum hardly ever disagreed with his step-dad.

Then Dominic's mobile rang. To his huge surprise it was Lara.

"Can you talk?" she said.

"Yeah."

"So did they really freak out?" she asked.

"My step-dad wanted to, but Mum sort of stopped him. She said it's not the end of the world."

"Your mum's growing up," Lara said.

"What about yours?" Dominic asked.

"My dad's not back yet. But my mum said she's going to walk me to school in the morning and then stand outside the school gates all day to make sure I don't try and escape again. She also said I'm grounded for ten years."

"Ten years?" Dominic repeated.

Lara snorted. "By tomorrow she'll be doing all her 'let's discuss our feelings' rubbish again. And anyway, all the time she was having a go at me I wanted to laugh. Do you know why?"

"No."

"Because of you."

"Me?" Dominic was amazed.

"Yeah," Lara said. "When I woke up today I was so not OK, but now … You're a really funny guy, Dominic."

"Yeah, I suppose I am," Dominic said, more to himself than Lara.

"So what are you doing tomorrow night?" Lara asked.

"Nothing."

"Well, I'll see you about seven o'clock," she said. "We can work out where we're going to meet up later."

"But I thought you were grounded," Dominic said.

"Oh, don't worry about that, Dom."

She'd called him Dom. Not Nerd Boy. Dom.

"You do want to see me tomorrow night, don't you?" she asked. She sounded a bit less sure of herself.

Dominic couldn't reply fast enough. "Yeah, of course I do. I was just a bit shocked you rang me – but shocked in a good way."

Lara laughed again and rang off.

Dominic stared at his mobile.

He had a date with the hottest girl at his school.

And a new name.

Meet Dom – Lara's boyfriend.

Now he was getting ahead of himself.

But it didn't matter how many detentions
Dom got at school – he couldn't wait for
tomorrow.

Our books are tested
for children and young people by
children and young people.

Thanks to everyone who consulted on
a manuscript for their time and effort in
helping us to make our books better
for our readers.